The Frog Prince was first published by the brothers Grimm in Germany,
in the early 19th century. In England it was first published by Robert Chambers in
1842, and was usually called *The Well of the World's End*. There is no fixed version of
the story, or of its ending. Sometimes the frog demands to be beheaded; sometimes the
princess throws him against a wall, hoping to kill him; sometimes the princess
sleeps with the frog, and after three nights grows to love him.

Text copyright © 1990 by Jan Ormerod and David Lloyd
Illustrations copyright © 1990 by Jan Ormerod
First published in Great Britain by Walker Books Ltd.
Printed in Hong Kong

First U.S. edition 1 2 3 4 5 6 7 8 9 10

Library of Congress Cataloging in Publication Data

Ormerod, Jan.   The frog prince / by Jan Ormerod.
p.   cm.   Summary: As payment for retrieving the princess's ball, the frog exacts a promise which the
princess is reluctant to fulfill. ISBN 0-688-09568-2. — ISBN 0-688-09569-0 (lib. bdg.)
[1. Fairy tales.   2. Folklore—Germany.]   I. Title. PZ8.0695Fr   1990   398.21′0943—dc20 [E]
89-12977 CIP AC

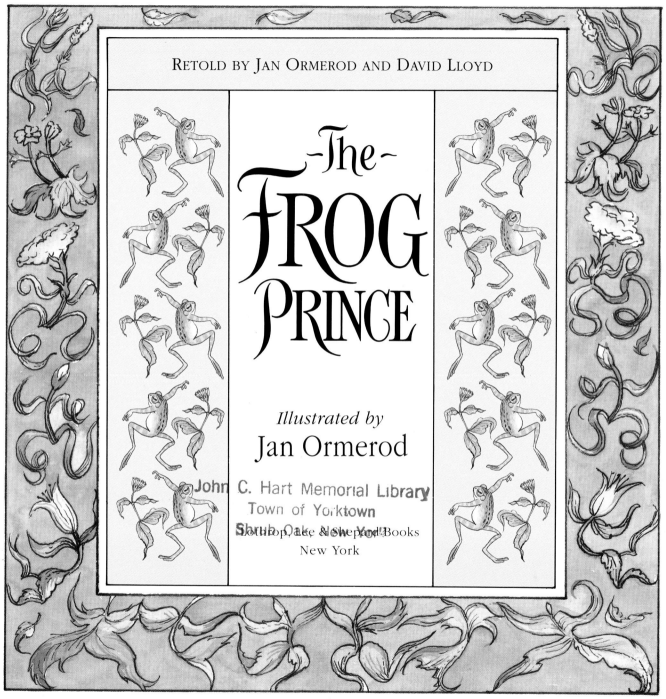

RETOLD BY JAN ORMEROD AND DAVID LLOYD

The FROG PRINCE

Illustrated by
Jan Ormerod

Lothrop, Lee & Shepard Books
New York

One summer evening a princess went down to the woods, playing with her golden ball. She threw it in the air and caught it. She threw it higher and caught it again. She threw it higher and higher until she dropped it, and it rolled and fell into a deep, dark pond.

The princess looked into the water, but she could not see the bottom and she could not see her ball. She began to cry, because the ball was her favorite toy.

While she was crying, a frog put its head out of the water and said,

"What is the matter,
my honey, my heart?
Why do you weep,
my own darling?"

Then the princess, still crying, told the frog how she had lost her ball.

"I will bring you back your ball," the frog said, "but only if you promise to love me, and let me be with you, and let me eat from your golden plate and sleep on your royal pillow."

So the princess promised, because the frog was just a frog, she thought.

The frog put its head down and dived under the water. And after a little while it came back up again with the ball and threw it on the ground.

The princess ran home with the ball as fast as she could, and she never thanked the frog or listened when it called after her, "Stop, princess, remember what you promised."

The next evening, as the princess sat down to dinner, she heard something coming up the marble staircase, and something tapped, tip tap, low down at the door. Then a voice said,

"Open the door,
my honey, my heart.
Open the door,
my own darling.
Remember the promise
you made in the woods.
Remember your promise
to love me."

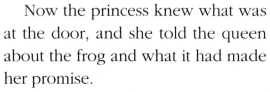

Now the princess knew what was at the door, and she told the queen about the frog and what it had made her promise.

"You must always keep your promises," the queen said. "Open the door." So the princess opened the door, and the frog hopped into the room, and the princess was terribly frightened.

The frog hopped close to the table, and it looked up at the princess with its great round eyes and said,

"Lift me to your knee,
    my honey, my heart.
Lift me to your knee,
    my own darling.
Remember the promise
    you made in the woods.
Remember your promise
    to love me."

Well, the princess did not like the idea of that at all, because the frog was wet, and a frog. But the queen told her again that promises must be kept, so she lifted the frog onto her lap, and though she went to sit by the fire, soon she felt as cold and miserable as can be.

For some time the princess and the frog sat like that, and the frog never said a word. But at last it spoke again.

"Let me eat from your plate,
my honey, my heart.
Let me eat from your plate,
my own darling.
Remember the promise
you made in the woods.
Remember your promise
to love me."

So now, because promises are made to be kept, the princess carried the frog to the table and fed it from her golden plate, with a little spoon, until the frog would eat no more.

Now the frog spoke again in its queer, croaking voice, and what it said made the princess shiver.

"Take me to bed,
my honey, my heart.
Take me to bed,
my own darling.
Remember the promise
you made in the woods.
Remember your promise
to love me."

And the princess shivered, because the frog was a cold, wet thing, but she took it in her hand and she took it up to bed, and all night it lay beside her on her royal pillow.

When dawn was beginning to break, the princess woke up, and the frog was still on her pillow. It stayed there for a while, but never said a word. Then it jumped up, hopped down the stairs, and left the palace. It has gone, thought the princess. I shall be troubled no more by the cold, wet thing. But she was wrong.

That night the frog came again. The princess heard it coming up the marble staircase; it tapped, tip tap, low down at the door; it sat on her lap and ate from her golden plate and slept all night on her royal pillow. And in the morning, when the princess woke, the frog was already leaving. He is a pretty sort of thing, she thought, though he is only a frog. Now he will trouble me no more. But she was wrong.

The third night the frog came as before, and everything happened as before, and for the third time the frog slept beside the princess all night long. And when the princess woke in the morning, she found herself sad and lonely, because the frog had already gone. She thought,

Where is my frog,
*   my honey, my heart?*
Where is my frog,
*   my own darling?*

Just then a voice spoke from the head of the bed, not the queer, croaking voice of the frog, but another, quite different voice.

"Here I am,
my honey, my heart.
Here I am,
my own darling."

And the princess saw, as soon as she looked, that the frog had become a prince, that the frog and the prince were the same, and she loved him.

In time the prince explained to the princess how he had been enchanted by a wicked witch, and how the princess had broken the spell. She had loved the prince as a frog, and three times—yes, three times—she had allowed the frog to sleep with her.

And in a little more time the prince and the princess were married, and as in all the best deep, dark, and royal stories, they lived happily ever after.

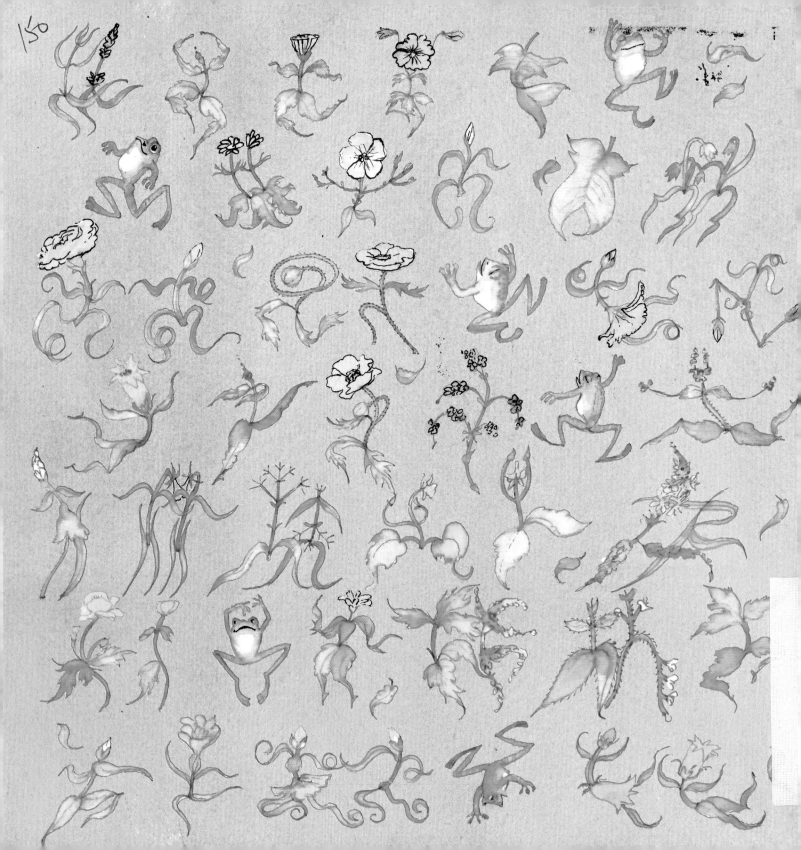

150